Hi there.

Are you good at solving problems?

OK, maybe there aren't any about at the moment. Not while all the people around you are flying high, with Virgin's cabin crew to take care of everything. But what about later on, after you've landed? Life on the ground is full of tricky little problems, isn't it? Like:

- What do you do if a cow gets stuck in your bathroom?
- How can you get chewing gum out of the cat's fur?
- What do you tell your bad-tempered grandmother when you realize you've baked her reading glasses into her birthday cake?
- How do you cope with fifteen toddlers covered in chocolate – in a room with a new white carpet?

When people are faced with problems like that, they need help! And, if you're a super-genius like me, you're probably itching to step in and tell them what to do.

BEWARE! DO NOTHING UNTIL YOU'VE READ THIS BOOK!!!

Take my advice. I know what I'm talking about. So lean back, while you have the chance, and read the whole story for yourself.

Your friend

Sophy Simpson
Rent-A-Genius
(Believe me, I know best!)

GILLIAN CROSS

Rent-a-Genius

Illustrated by Glenys Ambrus

PUFFIN BOOKS

PUFFIN BOOKS

Published by the Penguin Group
Penguin Books Ltd, 80 Strand, London WC2R 0RL, England
Penguin Putnam Inc., 375 Hudson Street, New York, New York 10014, USA
Penguin Books Australia Ltd, 250 Camberwell Road, Camberwell, Victoria 3124, Australia
Penguin Books Canada Ltd, 10 Alcorn Avenue, Toronto, Ontario, Canada M4V 3B2
Penguin Books India (P) Ltd, 11 Community Centre, Panchsheel Park, New Delhi – 110 017, India
Penguin Books (NZ) Ltd, Cnr Rosedale and Airborne Roads, Albany, Auckland, New Zealand
Penguin Books (South Africa) (Pty) Ltd, 24 Sturdee Avenue, Rosebank 2196, South Africa

Penguin Books Ltd, Registered Offices: 80 Strand, London WC2R 0RL, England

www.penguin.com

First published by Hamish Hamilton 1991
Published in Puffin Books 1993
2

This edition published exclusively for
Virgin Atlantic Airlines copyright © 2003

Text copyright © Gillian Cross, 1991
Illustrations copyright © Glenys Ambrus, 1991
All rights reserved

The moral right of the author and illustrator has been asserted

Set in Baskerville

Made and printed in England by Clays Ltd, St Ives plc

British Library Cataloguing in Publication Data
A CIP catalogue record for this book is available from
the British Library

ISBN 0–141–31764–7

1. *Other People's Problems*

SOPHY SIMPSON ALWAYS knew best. She
couldn't help it. She just noticed what
people were doing wrong. But when
she told them they never seemed to be
grateful.

She walked in while her father was
making a cake and, straightaway, she
spotted what was missing.

"Hang on, Dad. You ought to be
wearing an apron."

"What?" said her father. He turned
round, still holding the whirring mixer.

FLOOMPH! A huge blob of chocolate cake mixture flew on to his trousers.

"You *see*?" Sophy said. "Now if you'd been wearing an apron –"

But her father didn't put an apron on. He just glared at Sophy until she went away.

In the sitting room, her sister Alice was sitting on the sofa in her best dress, waiting to go to a party. She was stroking the cat and watching television. Sophy shook her head.

"Alice! You shouldn't have Pickles on your lap."

Alice didn't look round. "Go away, Sophy."

"But –"

"Go away, Sophy!"

"But I only wanted to say . . ."

"GO AWAY!!"

Sophy shrugged. "OK. Keep your hair on. I just thought you'd *like* to know that Pickles has muddy feet."

Alice jumped up with a yelp and pushed the cat on to the floor. But she didn't say thank you.

Sophy wandered upstairs. It was noisy up there, because her mother and her brother Ben were having an argument.

"If you don't pick up those dirty clothes this instant," Mrs Simpson shouted, "you can do your own washing from now on."

"I haven't got *time* to do it now!" Ben yelled back. "Look at this great heap of homework! I'll never finish it before Monday if I crawl round picking up clothes . . ."

"What makes you think I've got time to crawl round?" screeched Mrs Simpson.

"*You* haven't got any homework to do."

Sophy thought it was a stupid quarrel. If they were both short of time, why were they wasting so much of it shouting at each other? Quietly she slipped between the two of them.

4

They were so busy arguing that they didn't notice Sophy creeping round the room, picking up the dirty clothes.

She took the whole lot into the bathroom and dropped them into the dirty linen basket. Then she went back to Ben's bedroom and tugged at her mother's sleeve.

"Mum —"

"Go away, Sophy! Can't you see I'm busy?"

"But you don't need to go on arguing," Sophy said. "I've done it. I've picked up the dirty clothes."

Ben and Mrs Simpson stopped glaring at each other and looked round. But they didn't smile. They didn't look pleased at all. Instead, they both yelled at Sophy.

"What did you do that for? *He* was supposed to do it!"

6

"Why did you have to interfere?"

It was the last straw. Sophy stamped her foot and glared at them both.

"Everybody in this family is horrible! I keep trying to help, but all you do is shout at me."

"It wasn't any of your business!" Ben yelled. He went into his bedroom and slammed the door.

Mrs Simpson sighed. "I know you mean well, Sophy. But there is such a thing as being too clever."

"I'm not too clever." Sophy scowled. "I'm only trying to help."

Wearily, Mrs Simpson rubbed a hand across her forehead. "But we're happy as we are. Why don't you find someone who really *needs* help?"

"All right!" Sophy said fiercely. "I will!" She marched into her bedroom,

slammed the door and sat down at her
desk.

Find someone who really needs help, her
mother had said. She liked the idea.
But she had to work out how to do
it . . .

For a moment or two she sat staring
at the desk. Then a big smile spread
across her face. Opening her cupboard,
she found a large sheet of white paper
and a black felt pen. Carefully, in
clear, neat letters, she wrote out a
poster.

RENT-A-GENIUS

Got a problem?
Sophy Simpson will solve it for you.
Only 50p a problem!
Satisfaction, or your money back!

It looked splendid. All she needed now was some advertising leaflets. If she put those through people's doors, everyone around would know about *Rent-A-Genius*. She began to copy out the words again, on small sheets of paper.

She meant to make a hundred

leaflets, but after twenty her wrist was aching. And twenty ought to be enough, anyway. That made one for every house in the road, and there were three or four people in most of the houses. Even if only half the people had problems, she would be very busy.

Stacking the leaflets into a neat pile, she took them, and the poster, and her sellotape and slipped quietly downstairs.

Alice was in the kitchen, moaning about the paw marks on her dress. But Mrs Simpson wasn't listening, because she was complaining about the chocolate cake mixture on the kitchen walls. And Mr Simpson was trying to find out why she and Ben had been shouting at each other.

Sophy grinned to herself. Let them get on with it. She slipped out of the front door, shut it silently behind her and went off to advertise *Rent-A-Genius*.

The poster looked very good on the garden gate. Several people stopped to read it while she was sticking it up, but none of them seemed to have problems. They just smiled at Sophy and walked on.

Oh well, at least that gave her time to deliver the leaflets. Briskly she walked up one side of the road and down the other, pushing them through letterboxes.

She was just walking back home, after delivering the last leaflet, when she saw a strange sight coming down the road.

It was Paul.

Or was it? It was Paul's face, certainly, but the rest was all wrong. Outside school, Paul always wore torn jeans, an old tee-shirt and dirty trainers. And a big grin.

This boy was dressed in a smart, tight suit, with a sparkling clean shirt. His shoes shone, his hair was brushed flat and his bow-tie seemed to be strangling him. He looked utterly miserable.

"Paul?" called Sophy.

He looked round. "Oh. Hello, Sophy." But he didn't smile.

"What's up? Why are you wearing those clothes?"

Paul shuddered. "Don't ask. I don't want to talk about it."

Sophy looked at him again, and suddenly her eyes lit up. This was *it*. "Paul," she said gently, "have you got a problem?"

Paul pulled a face. "I certainly have."

"Well, you're talking to the right person. Look over there, on my gate."

Paul turned his head and read the words of Sophy's poster.

"Rent-A-Genius? What does that mean?"

"It means," Sophy said firmly, "that I'm going to solve your problem. Come inside and let's talk about it."

"But there's nothing you can do —"

"I bet there is." Sophy grabbed his arm and began to steer him towards her house.

"And anyway, I haven't got fifty pence –"

That made Sophy hesitate. But only for a second. "You can be free," she said. "Because you're my first customer."

She pushed him into her front garden and pulled the gate shut behind them.

2. *Double Trouble*

"SIT THERE," SOPHY said, "and wait for me."

She pushed Paul into the sitting room and shut the door. Then she went upstairs and fetched a notebook, a rubber and three sharp pencils.

When she came back, he was standing by the window, looking even more miserable than before.

"I can't stay long," he muttered. "I shall get into the most terrible trouble if I don't find –"

"There's not going to be any trouble," Sophy said. "Trust me."

She sat down in the biggest armchair, opened her notebook and wrote a neat heading at the top of the first page.

Customer No. *1 – PAUL*

"Now," she said, "what's the problem?"

"It's not just one problem," Paul said gloomily. "I've got TWO."

"Two problems?"

"Two grandmothers." Paul pulled an even worse face and sat down opposite Sophy. "And they're both coming to tea today."

"Oh, I see." Sophy grinned. "That's why you're dressed up like that."

"S'right. They reckon I ought to be

a dear little boy with clean hands and good manners. You should hear how they go on at my mum if they catch me in my jeans. Whenever they come, I have to have my hair cut and my nails cleaned and I have to wear these *dumb* clothes."

Paul tweaked his bow-tie furiously. Then he got up to look in the mirror so that he could straighten it again.

Sophy frowned. "It sounds pretty dreadful – but it's not exactly a problem. You *are* dressed up. You *do* look like a dear little boy. All you have to do is stick it out until the end of the day."

"That's no trouble," Paul said. "I'm used to it. But they want something extra today."

That sounded more interesting. Sophy sat up straight, smoothed out her notebook and wrote, *Visiting grandmothers want* underneath the heading.

"So what do they want?"

"Huh!" Paul laughed, bitterly. "They want to meet my friends." He put on a mincing, quavery voice, like a complaining old lady. *"Wouldn't it be nice if some of Paulie's dear little friends came to tea while we were there."* And then, in a deeper, bossier voice he added, *"Yes, that would be splendid! We'd like to meet your chums, Paul."*

Sophy chuckled. "Well, you've got lots of *chums*. Ask some of them round. They won't mind."

"Don't be thick! Think what my friends are like!"

Sophy thought. Slugger Jackson. Masher White. Jock the Biker. Tes Wilson. "Hmmph," she said.

"You see?" Paul said hopelessly. "If *they* turn up, my grans will go mad. They'll be horrible to Mum. And she cries."

Sophy frowned. "They're not exactly dear little boys. But they must have got best clothes. Wouldn't they clean themselves up for you? Just for one afternoon?"

"Like who?" said Paul.

"Well – what about Slugger Jackson?"

"Haven't you seen him this week? He's got the world's biggest black eye."

"Oh. Yes." Sophy couldn't argue with that. It was enormous. "Well, what about Masher White?"

"*Two* black eyes. Who do you think Slugger was fighting?" Paul said impatiently.

"Jock isn't a fighter, though. Why don't you try him?"

Paul looked at Sophy as though she were an idiot. "Jock's underneath his brother's Yamaha, of course. They always take the bike to bits at weekends. It would take about six hours to get the oil off him."

"Well —"

"And I can't ask Tes either, because he always knocks things over. It would be tea and jam tarts all over the floor if he came." Paul shook his head and stood up. "Honestly, Sophy, it's no good. There's nothing you can do. Mum sent me out to find someone, but I'll just have to go back and tell her –"

"Sit down!" said Sophy. Paul was her first customer. She wasn't going to let him go until she had solved his problem. "Just let me *think* for a minute."

She shut her eyes and pressed her fingertips against her forehead. Paul shuffled his feet restlessly, but she didn't take any notice of that. She was going to solve his problem.

She concentrated harder – and a big grin spread across her face.

"Got it!"

Grabbing her pencil, she wrote a list.

> *Nice Clean Children*
> Mary-Anne Carrington
> Selina Sotherby
> Jeremy Phillips
> Alan Noakes

Paul peered over her shoulder as she wrote. "Yuck!" he said. "Yuck, yuck and *yuck*!"

Sophy grinned. "Don't be rude about your dear little friends who are coming to tea this afternoon."

"Oh Soph! I can't ask any of them. They're poison!"

"They're nice, clean children," Sophy said primly. "And they'll be glad to come to tea with you, I bet. Nobody ever asks them."

"Of course they don't," Paul

snorted. "Of all the boring, smarmy teacher's pets . . ."

"But your grandmothers will think they're sweet. Won't they?"

"We–ell –"

"You've got to be practical," said Sophy. "Why don't you go round and ask them straightaway? Start with Alan and Jeremy."

"They won't believe me," Paul muttered. "They'll think it's a plot to beat them up."

Sophy thought about it. If she were Jeremy – or Alan – would she trust Paul? Hmm. "Perhaps I'd better ask them. I bet I can get them to come."

"Do you think you could?"

"I'm sure I can," Sophy said briskly. "What time do you want them at your house?"

"Four o'clock."

"Fine." Sophy wrote a note in her book, to remind herself.

4 pm. Nice clean children to arrive at Paul's.

Then she closed the book with a snap and stood up. "Don't worry. Your problem is in the hands of Rent-A-Genius. And everything will be fine."

"Well . . ."

Paul still looked doubtful. But before he could say anything else there was a thunderous knocking on the door. A loud, shrill voice called through the letterbox.

"Sophy! Sophy, are you there?"

3.   A Spot of Bother

"SOMEONE ANSWER THE door!" shrieked Mrs Simpson. She was upstairs, ironing Alice's other party dress.

"Stop the noise!" bellowed Mr Simpson from the kitchen, where he was scrubbing the walls.

Even Ben stopped doing his homework long enough to yell. "Sophy! Hurry up!"

Sophy ran and opened the door, with Paul close behind her. Outside stood a figure dressed in a thick school

26

mackintosh. Her hood was pulled well up and a scarf was wrapped round her face.

"Maria?" Sophy stared. "Aren't you terribly hot?"

Maria's eyes gleamed above the edge of the scarf. "Get rid of *him*!" she muttered, pointing at Paul.

"He's just going." Sophy gave Paul a little push, so that he stepped through the door. "'Bye, Paul."

Paul looked back at her. "But –"

"I've solved your problem," Sophy said impatiently. "It's Maria's turn now."

"But –"

Sophy gave him another little push. "Four o'clock. OK? I *promise*."

Paul hesitated for a moment. Then he shrugged and headed off down the road. Immediately, Maria seized

Sophy's arm and dragged her into the house.

"You've got to help me!" she hissed. "I'll be a joke! I'll be a laughing-stock! I'll never be able to live it down!"

"Hang on, hang on." Sophy unwound Maria's fingers from her arm. "Let's be business-like."

She pushed Maria into the sitting room, sat down and headed the second page in her notebook.

Customer No. 2 – *MARIA*

As she wrote, Maria prowled round
the room, with her hood still up and
her scarf still tightly wound round her
face.

"Why don't you sit down?" Sophy
said. "Take off your coat and things.
You must be roasting."

"Not yet! Not yet!" Maria rolled her
eyes dramatically towards the ceiling.

"Let's hear it then." Sophy tapped
her pencil against the paper. "I'm
ready. What's the problem?"

"Disaster!" Maria clapped her
hands to her forehead and flung herself
onto the couch, next to Sophy. She
grabbed Sophy's arm, and spoke in a
hushed whisper. "This evening, it's the
Dancing School Summer Show.
Right?"

"If you say so." Sophy didn't go to the Dancing School, but she knew it was the most important thing in Maria's life. "Aren't you in the show?"

"Of course I am," said Maria. "But in a ridiculous part. Have they made me a princess? No! Have they made me a swan? No! Have they – ?"

"OK, OK." Sophy tried not to sound impatient. "What *have* they made you?"

Maria closed her eyes and spoke in a deep, tragic voice. "A pig."

"A *pig*?" said Sophy.

"A PIG!"

Sophy struggled to keep a straight face. "I can't do anything about that, you know. It's up to the Dancing School what part you have."

"Of course, of course!" Maria flapped her hand impatiently. "And if

I refuse to be the pig, they will *never* let
me be the princess. So I have been
making the best of it."

"You have?" Sophy couldn't
imagine how.

"Of course I have." Maria flung her
arms wide. "I am the best – the most
delightful – the *prettiest* pig in the whole
show." She closed her eyes and smiled.
"In all the rehearsals, I was more
charming than the princess herself."

"Hmm," said Sophy. "So what's the
problem?"

31

"This!" shrieked Maria.

Suddenly and violently, she pulled off her scarf and threw back the hood of her mackintosh. There on her face were three large red spots, two on her left cheek and one on her right.

"Spots!" she said, shuddering. "I never have spots. You know I never have spots. And now – today of all days – it is a DISASTER!"

"But they're only spots," said Sophy. "Does it really matter?"

"Of course it matters!" Maria yelled. "It's difficult enough to be a charming, delightful pig. How will I ever manage it if I have spots? People will *laugh* at me."

"Some pigs do have spots –" Sophy started to say. But then she saw Maria's face. She stopped quickly and wrote in her notebook instead.

Problem: spots on face.
Solution:

She didn't have to waste any time thinking about that. It was easy. If all her problems were that simple, she

33

was going to make a lot of money.

"Calm down, Maria," she said. "And I'll tell you what to do."

"Yes! Yes!" Maria turned and stared at Sophy with big, round eyes.

"Go down to the chemist," Sophy said, "and buy some cover-up cream. Got that?"

"Cover-up cream," Maria repeated carefully.

"That's right. Then bring it back here, and I'll put some on for you. And no one will ever know about the spots. Honestly."

Maria grabbed Sophy's hand and squeezed it. "Are you sure it will work?"

"Of course it will. I've watched Alice doing it, loads of times."

"Brilliant!"

Maria jumped up, pulled on her

mackintosh hood and wrapped the scarf three times round the bottom part of her face. Then she waved at Sophy and slid out through the door.

Grinning, Sophy filled in the last word of her notes on Customer Number 2.

Solution: cover-up cream.

Then she flipped back to the page before. Paul's problem still wasn't solved. She stared down at the list of names. Mary-Anne Carrington, Selina Sotherby, Jeremy Phillips and Alan Noakes. Where was the best place to start? At Alan's, perhaps. He was *always* at home. And if she telephoned –

But before she could pick up the phone the doorbell rang and the voices started yelling again.

"Sophy!"

"Answer the door!"

"Can you get that, Soph?"

"SOPHEEE!"

"OK," Sophy called back. "I'm on my way."

She opened the door. Outside was Ryan Shaw, one of the boys from the top class. He had a bulging carrier bag in his left hand.

Sophy was surprised. "Hello, Ryan."

"Are you Rent-A-Genius?" Ryan said briskly.

Sophy nodded.

"Great." Ryan put a hand into his pocket, pulled out fifty pence and thrust it at Sophy. "Got a problem for you."

4. Dirty Work

FOR A SECOND, Sophy stared up at him with her mouth open. Ryan had a problem for her? *Ryan*? The biggest, strongest, bossiest boy in the whole school?

"Well?" He shook the money under her nose. "Are you going to take it? Or is this whole Rent-A-Genius thing just a joke?"

"N-no," Sophy said faintly. "It's not a joke." She took the money and put it in her pocket. "Come in here."

As she followed Ryan through the sitting room door, she took a deep breath. By the time they were both sitting down, she had gathered her wits again.

"Right," she said. "Let me put you in my records."

"Why do you need to fuss around?" said Ryan. "It's a very simple problem."

"I've still got to be efficient." Sophy sharpened her pencil and began to write.

Customer No. 3 – RYAN

Then she looked up and smiled at him. "Now. What's the trouble?"

"This," Ryan said shortly.

He picked up his plastic carrier bag and turned it upside down. Out fell a stream of muddy clothes, all over the

carpet. There were two pairs of shorts, two shirts and at least four pairs of stiff, smelly socks. Bits of dried mud flaked off them and scattered all over the carpet.

"Hey! What are you doing?" Sophy said.

Ryan grinned. "Well, you wanted to know about the problem."

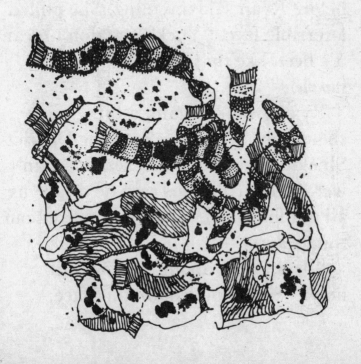

"But that doesn't mean I want it all over the carpet." Sophy leaned forward and took a closer look. "Anyway, what's it doing in that state? It's football kit, isn't it? This isn't the football season."

"We start next week," said Ryan.

"So why is all your stuff dirty now?" But Sophy had realised the answer before Ryan said anything. She pulled a terrible face. "Yuck! You don't mean it's been like that *all through the summer*?"

Ryan grinned again, a bit sheepishly. "Well, we won the District Shield at the end of last season, didn't we? And Mr Phillips said he'd take us all out for lunch. So we just shoved our things away –"

"And forgot about them? Until now?" Sophy pulled another face.

"That's pretty disgusting. But it's not a problem. They'll just have to be washed."

"Ah!" Ryan said. "Well, that's just it. When our mums saw the kit, they all went on strike. Said there was no way they were going to wash it."

Sophy looked down at the dirty clothes again. "So?" She still didn't see the problem.

"So we'll all get chucked off the team," Ryan said impatiently. "That's one of the things Mr Phillips is really strict about. Anyone who turns up with dirty kit is *out*."

Sophy shrugged. "So what do you want me to do about it?"

"I want you to wash it, of course."

"*Wash it?*" Sophy almost shrieked the words. "Why should *I* wash your filthy, disgusting football kit?"

43

Ryan reached into his pocket, pulled out one of Sophy's leaflets and slapped it down on the table. "Look at that. It says, *Got a problem? Sophy Simpson will solve it for you*. Well, this is my problem and you've taken my fifty pence. You'll *have* to solve it."

"I'm not taking in washing," Sophy snapped. "I solve problems with my *brain*, you great thickhead."

"It doesn't say that on your leaflet. I could get you into trouble, under the Trades Descriptions Act –"

"My leaflet doesn't say I'll do your washing. It just says I'll solve your problem."

"Go on then," Ryan said tauntingly. "Solve it. What are you going to do? Persuade my mum to change her mind?"

"Certainly not! She's quite right. It's

your own fault that kit's so disgusting.
I wouldn't wash it if I were her."

"So what're you going to do then,
genius?"

"It's perfectly simple," Sophy said.
"You'll have to wash it yourself."

"*Me?*" Ryan looked horrified.

Sophy would have laughed if she hadn't been so angry. "That's right. *You* got it dirty. *You* wash it."

"But I can't –"

"Why not?"

"You can't expect me to –"

"Why *not*?"

"Well if you must know –" Ryan suddenly stopped shouting. He looked down and shuffled his feet. "– I don't know how."

"There's nothing to know. You've only got to bung them in the washing machine. You might have to do it twice over, with the state they're in. Or even three times. But they should come clean in the end."

"Can't work the washing machine, can I?" Ryan muttered. "My mum won't let me near it."

"Go to the launderette then."

"I've only got fifty pence." He looked up triumphantly. "And I gave that to *you*, didn't I, cleverclogs? So –"

"Wait!"

Sophy shut her eyes and thought fast. Ryan had a problem all right. But she wasn't going to be bullied into doing his horrible washing. There had to be another way . . .

"Got it!" She opened her eyes again and grinned. "It's perfectly simple. I won't *do* the washing for you, but I'll teach you how to do it. I'll give you a washing machine lesson in my mum's washing machine.''

"We-ell."

"It's that or nothing. If you don't like it, you can have your money back.'' Sophy held out the fifty pence.

Ryan thought it over for a moment and then he nodded. "OK, you can give me a lesson. Now?"

Sophy flipped through her notebook and worked it out. Customers seemed to be piling up. She had to find those people for Paul's tea party before four o'clock and it was already after three. And Maria would be back with the cover-up cream in a moment or two.

"I can't do it right away," she said. "But if you come back at four o'clock I should be ready."

"Fine." Ryan turned and headed for the door. "I'll be there."

"Hang on a minute!" Sophy yelled. "You can't leave all those muddy clothes on the carpet! My mum'll go bananas."

He didn't come back, so she scooped them up and ran after him. He was at the gate before she managed to catch him.

"Take it with you!" she said firmly, pushing the whole lot into his arms.

"All right, all right, keep your hair on." Ryan pushed the clothes into the carrier bag and strolled through the gate with a cheery wave. "See you at four."

"Phew!"

Sophy closed her eyes for a second as he walked off. Bossing him around had been quite a strain. And she couldn't waste any time recovering. She had to think about visitors for Paul, and cover-up cream, and washing machine lessons. The first thing was to get to the telephone . . .

But as she turned to go back into the house, a body came flying over the fence beside her. Someone crashed straight into her and grabbed hold of her arm.

"Sophy, you've got to help me!" muttered a desperate voice, in her ear. "I don't know what I'm going to do. Mum will *slaughter* me!"

50

5. *The Tomato Disaster*

SOPHY SAT DOWN suddenly, in the middle of the path, and the flying body overbalanced and fell on top of her.

"What's going on?" she gasped.

"Sorry," muttered the body. It sat up and untangled itself from Sophy. "I didn't mean to knock you over."

Sophy stared. It was Natalie, the new girl from next door. Quiet, calm-looking Natalie.

"I don't want to be a nuisance," mumbled Natalie. She twisted her

hands together and looked miserable.
"It's just that – I don't know what to
do! And you've got that notice on your
gate. Are you terribly busy?"

Sophy stood up and dusted herself
off. "Well I am, actually. I've got to do
some make-up and find people for a
tea party and run a washing machine
lesson –"

Natalie's bottom lip trembled. "Oh.
Sorry. I didn't mean to –"

She began to back away. But Sophy
couldn't let her go like that. She
wanted to know what was happening.

It must be something really dreadful, to send a quiet girl like that leaping over the fence.

"You've got a problem, have you?"

"It's not just a problem," Natalie said tearfully. "It's – oh, you'll have to come and see."

Grabbing Sophy's hand, she pulled her across the rose bed, over the fence and into the next door house.

"Mum left me to look after Henry while she went to the shops. She said she'd be quick but it's been *ages* – and he's been an absolute horror, all the afternoon – and I started to clear up – and while I wasn't watching him –"

Natalie shuddered, pushed Sophy into her house and pulled the front door shut. Sophy looked round.

"Wow!" she said. "I can see why your mum's going to be furious."

The hall looked like a ploughed field. All the pot plants that stood at the bottom of the stairs had been pulled over. The carpet was covered with earth and leaves, and someone had trodden wet earth round and round and up the stairs.

But Natalie didn't seem to be bothered. "That? Oh, that's nothing. Mum'll just shove the plants back in the pots. But up *here* –"

She tugged Sophy towards the stairs and led the way up. The bathroom was at the top of the stairs, and Sophy gasped as she looked through the open door.

There were wet towels everywhere. Someone had squeezed toothpaste over the toilet seat and drawn pictures on the mirror with soap. The plug was in the basin and the water was gently overflowing on to a heap of books on the floor.

Sophy leaped to the taps and switched them off. Then she pulled out the plug. As the water drained away, she found a cloth and began to clean off the toothpaste.

Natalie looked puzzled. "What are you doing?"

"There's no point in giving up," said Sophy briskly. "It's a terrible mess, but we can get it clear before your mum comes home. If we work fast."

"But we don't want to waste time on that. Mum never minds Henry having a bit of fun in the bathroom. If he thinks the bathroom's a jolly place, he's more likely to wash. That's what she always says."

Sophy swallowed hard. "You mean –

this isn't what you brought me in here to see?"

"Of course not. Oh come on, Sophy!"

Sophy dropped the cloth and stood up slowly. She couldn't imagine anything much worse than the bathroom. Whatever Natalie was taking her to see must be absolutely horrible.

She felt rather nervous as she followed along the landing. There seemed to be something wrong with all the other rooms they passed as well.

In Natalie's room, there was a huge pile of books and papers, with talcum powder sprinkled all over them.

In her parents' bedroom, all the clothes had been pulled out of the drawers and scattered over the floor.

And from Henry's little bedroom

56

came a faint chuckling sound. When
Sophy glanced in, she saw Henry
sitting up in the cot with his teddy
bear, shaking tomato ketchup on to the
sheets.

"Natalie —" Sophy said faintly.

But Natalie hardly looked round.
"You stay there, Henry!" she called as
she passed. "You're not getting up
until Mum comes home."

"Bed," Henry said cheerfully. "Ted.
Head."

"Red bedspread," muttered Sophy,
looking at the ketchup. She took a deep

breath and followed Natalie to the last door at the end of the landing. Whatever was in there must be unspeakable.

Natalie turned the handle and flung the door wide open. "Now!" she said. "What am I going to do about this?"

Sophy stepped inside – and looked round in amazement. There was no mess at all. The room was bare and tidy and almost completely empty, with no carpet and no pictures on the walls.

At one end was an artist's easel, with an unfinished painting on it. It faced a small table. Arranged on the table were a bowl full of fruit, a small vase of flowers and a plate.

An empty plate.

It was impossible to guess what was upsetting Natalie. But obviously

something was. Whipping out her
notebook, Sophy flicked to the fourth
page and wrote a heading.

Customer No. 4 – NATALIE

"Tell me about it," she said.

Natalie closed her eyes for a
moment. Then she walked across to
the table. "See these things? The plate
and the flowers and the bowl?"

Sophy nodded.

"They're Mum's still life
arrangement," Natalie said. "For the

competition at her art school. She terribly wants to win. She spent *three days* just arranging all this before she even began to paint it. She only started the actual picture last night."

"Yes?" Sophy said. "So?"

Natalie took another deep breath and pointed at the plate. "It's empty," she said, in a small, tight voice. "They've gone, and the arrangement's ruined. Henry *ate* them."

"Ate what?" said Sophy.

"The tomatoes. All three of them."

"Tomatoes?" Sophy nearly laughed out loud. "For heaven's sake, Nat, what's all the fuss about? I'll look after Henry while you go and buy some more tomatoes. And your mum will never know."

"Of course she will!"

"But how –"

"Because they were YELLOW tomatoes!" Natalie wailed. "Mum had to hunt everywhere for them. I think they were the last three in the town. I'll never find any more!"

Sophy looked at the empty plate. "Can't she have red tomatoes instead?"

"Of course she can't!" sniffed Natalie. "Don't be so stupid, Sophy! The whole picture is made up of different shades of yellow. You can't just plonk three great red blobs into the middle of it."

She was right. The creamy yellow fruit bowl was full of lemons and yellowish-green grapes. The plate was white, with a yellow rim, and the cloth draped over the table was made of old, yellowed lace. Red tomatoes

61

would look simply dreadful.

But where on earth were they going to get yellow ones from? Sophy frowned and shut her eyes, trying to think of a solution.

"Mum's going to get back any minute," muttered Natalie desperately. "She said she'd be here by three, and it's almost four already."

Something niggled at the back of Sophy's brain. "Almost four?"

"Well, it's ten to."

Ten to four. . . ? Ten to FOUR!

Sophy yelped and opened her eyes. She was supposed to have found some people for Paul's tea party by four o'clock. She'd *promised*.

"What's the matter, Soph?" Natalie peered at her. "You look peculiar."

Sophy didn't answer. She had ten minutes. It was no use trying to phone anyone now. It would take too long to explain. There was only one solution.

"Sophy?"

She would have to go herself!

By the time she had worked it out, she was already halfway to the door. It was a pity she didn't have a smart dress on, but at least her jeans were clean. And she'd just washed her hair –

"Sophy!" Natalie called after her. "What about the yellow tomatoes?"

"I'll be back!" Sophy shouted, from the bottom of the stairs.

"But that's no good –"

Sophy wrenched open the front door. Out of the corner of her eye, she saw Natalie at the top of the stairs, with Henry tucked under one arm. But there was no time to think about that.

She had to get to Paul's!

6. Nice Little Friends

"SOPHY! COME BACK! You can't just run off!"

Sophy heard Natalie's voice, quite clearly, but she had no breath left to answer. First things first. She had *promised* Paul that someone would be at his house by four o'clock. Everything else would have to wait until later.

She turned left, up the road – and saw Maria heading straight for her, still wrapped up in her mac and scarf.

"I've got the stuff!" Maria shouted,

64

waving a tube. "And we've just got time to do it."

"Back soon!" Sophy panted as she got nearer to Maria. "Go into my house – wait –"

Maria looked horrified. "But that'll be *much* too late. Sophy, you've got to –"

Sophy looked left and right, took a deep breath and swerved across the road. Behind her, she could hear Maria's yell of fury mixed with the sound of Natalie's running feet, but there was no time to stop and sort it out. Surely they could wait half an hour . . .

She zoomed round the corner – and almost bumped into Ryan.

And not only Ryan. He had the rest of the football team with him. When they saw Sophy, they all grinned and

waved muddy carrier bags at her.

"Good old Sophy!"

"Here she is!"

"Going to give us a lesson too, Soph?"

They stood round her in a circle, looking very large. Sophy remembered that she still had Ryan's fifty pence in her pocket. And she *had* promised to give him a lesson at four o'clock.

But then she had promised Paul as well . . .

Thinking furiously, she flashed a
brilliant smile at the football team. "Of
course I'll teach you all. Just go to my
house and wait for me."

"Wait for you?" Ryan said. "But
you promised –"

At that instant, Maria came racing
round the corner, yelling, "Sophy,
you've got to come back NOW!"

Close behind her was Natalie, with
Henry still tucked under one arm. She
hadn't got enough breath to say
anything except, "So-phy!"

Automatically, the footballers turned
to see what was happening. Seizing her
chance, Sophy ducked under Ryan's
arm and dodged out of sight, down the
alley that led into Paul's road. As she
ran, she heard Ryan mutter, "What's
going on?" And then, in a louder voice,
"Hey! Sophy! Where are you?"

It didn't take him long to work it out. Before Sophy reached the end of the alley, she heard him yell. "What about my fifty pence!"

Thirteen pairs of feet began to run after her, down the alley. Sophy took a deep breath and ran faster. Not far now. She was nearly at Paul's house.

She swerved round another corner, hearing the feet come closer and closer all the time, flung open Paul's garden

gate and almost fell against the
doorbell.

At the same moment, all the others
reached the gate and crowded into the
garden. As Paul's mother opened the
door, everyone began to shout.

"What on earth – ?"

"What about my fifty pence?"

"It's nearly time for the show –"

"The tomatoes –"

Sophy turned away from them all
and gave Paul's mother a bright,
beaming smile.

"Rent-A-Genius here. Paul wanted
some of his friends to come to tea."

"Yes. Well." Paul's mother
swallowed hard and looked nervously
over her shoulder. Before she could say
any more, a huge, bossy voice boomed
out from the sitting room.

"Paul, your little friends are here!"

And a thin, sharp voice croaked, "Go and bring them in, dear."

The sitting room door opened. "Come in," said Paul, while he was still behind it. "We've got a lovely chocolate cake."

A split second later, he saw the crowd in the doorway and his mouth dropped open. But by then it was too late. As soon as he said, "Chocolate cake", the footballers had started to charge in. They pushed Sophy and sent her staggering forward, across the little hall and into the sitting room.

"Hello, dear –" began the sharp, quavering voice.

"Pleased to meet you –" began the big, booming voice.

The two grandmothers sat side by side, one large and red-faced and the other small and neat. As Sophy

70

stumbled in, in her jeans and her tee-shirt, their smiles vanished. Up went their eyebrows.

"Well!" boomed the big grandmother.

"Goodness gracious!" muttered the small grandmother.

Sophy flopped into a chair, pushed off her feet by the people behind. "G-good afternoon," she panted.

The next person through the door was Natalie. As she stepped into the room, Henry wriggled out of her arms. Diving forward, he headed for the plates of cake spread out on the coffee table.

"Look out!" bellowed the big grandmother.

"Careful!" squeaked the small grandmother.

But it was too late. Henry was

already grabbing at the plates. Four of them slithered off the table, scattering crumbs everywhere. Then a cup of tea went flying. All over the big grandmother.

"Well really!" said the small grandmother. "I should have thought –"

But no one heard what she would have thought, because the football team burst into the room, with cries of joy.

"Hello, folks!"

"Smashing tea!"

"Chocolate cake, eh?"

They flopped into armchairs, tossing their carrier bags on to the floor. Heaps of muddy clothes spilled out on to the carpet.

Both the grandmothers leaped to their feet with cries of disgust.

"This is too much!" roared the big grandmother.

"Washing? In the *lounge*?" shrieked the small grandmother.

It was a disaster. Sophy just wanted
to close her eyes and pretend she
wasn't there. But she had promised
Paul that she would make things all
right with his grandmothers. So she
ought to try, even though things looked
hopeless.

"If you'll just let me explain –" she
started to say, in a tiny, polite voice.

But before she could get any further,
Maria came through the sitting room
door. Her hood had fallen off her head
and she must have dropped her scarf
somewhere while she was chasing
Sophy.

Both the grandmothers took one
look at her and stepped backwards.
Together, at the tops of their voices,
they screamed.

"CHICKENPOX!!!"

7.   *Problems Solved*

EVERYONE IN THE room turned to look at Maria. It was true. Instead of three rather small spots, she had hundreds. Her whole face was covered in them.

Both the grandmothers looked terrified.

"I've never had chickenpox!" boomed the big grandmother.

"I've had it THREE TIMES," squeaked the small grandmother, "and I don't want it again."

They backed away from Maria, into the kitchen.

"Oh dear!" muttered Paul's mother, going after them. "Wait a minute –"

But they didn't seem to be waiting at all. The back door opened and Paul's mother followed them out into the garden, still trying to apologise.

Paul scowled. "I bet they're going on at her out there. I bet they're making her *cry*. And it's all your fault, Sophy."

"I'm sorry," Sophy mumbled. "I did the best I could, but –"

"The best you could?" Paul looked round the room. "You've got to be joking!"

The football team were sitting with their feet on the coffee table, eating chocolate cake. Natalie was trying to stop Henry smearing butter on the carpet. And Maria was standing with her back to everyone, staring at her spots in the mirror.

"If that's the best you could do –" Paul said.

But he didn't get any further, because his mother walked back into the room. And she wasn't crying. She didn't even look sad. She was beaming all over her face.

Paul stared at her. "Mum? What happened?"

His mother's grin got even bigger. "They've decided that you're a wonderful, clean, well-behaved boy. They said they didn't realise how awful other children were."

"Cheek!" muttered the football team, with their mouths full of chocolate cake.

Paul's mother chuckled. "And they gave me these to give to you."

She held out two five pound notes. Paul looked down at them and his mouth fell open. So did everyone else's.

Sophy got her breath back first. "There you are!" she said briskly. "I've solved your problem, haven't I? Your grandmothers will always be pleased with you in future. Now they've seen the rest of us."

"Yes," said Paul. He sounded dazed. "Great, Sophy. Brilliant."

Ryan swallowed a gigantic piece of chocolate cake and wiped the crumbs away with the back of his hand. "Never mind about *his* problem. What about ours, Sophy? You promised –"

"Problem?" Paul's mother looked round at the football team, who were still munching chocolate cake. "What's your problem?"

"This," Ryan said. He stirred the dirty clothes with his foot and Henry shrieked in delight.

"Mud!"

"No!" wailed Natalie, as he picked up an armful of football socks. "Put them down!"

She started to pull them out of his hands and Paul's mother looked puzzled. "Why are those a problem? Can't you just wash them?"

"Don't know how to use the washing machine," said Ryan, with a smug glance at Sophy.

Paul's mother gasped. "At your age! That's terrible. It's high time you learned." She waved her hand at the dirty clothes. "Take all those into the kitchen and Paul will teach you what to do. Won't you, Paul?"

"Mmm? Yes. Of course."

Still looking dazed and clutching his five pound notes, Paul led the way into the kitchen. His mother watched the football team until they had picked up all the clothes and followed him. Then she shut the kitchen door after them.

Another problem solved, thought Sophy. But what about Natalie. . . ?

That looked hopeless. Natalie had just launched herself across the room to get hold of Henry again. He was rooting down beside an armchair. As Natalie reached him, he pulled up a bulging shopping bag.

"No, Henry! Put that down!" screeched Natalie.

Paul's mother looked round. "Oh, you can let him have those. None of us like them. One of Paul's grandmothers grew them in her garden."

"It's not something precious?" said Natalie.

Paul's mother grinned again. "What's precious about four pounds of yellow tomatoes?"

Natalie almost dropped the bag. "Four pounds?"

"*Yellow* tomatoes?" said Sophy.

"Why not?" Paul's mother looked puzzled. "Haven't you seen them before?"

"Oh, I have," breathed Natalie. "I *have*. But I thought I was never going to see them again."

She marched across the room and hugged Sophy.

"Brilliant! If it weren't for you, I'd never have found them." Then she grabbed Henry in one hand and the

tomatoes in the other. "Come on, Hen.
Let's see if we can get back before
Mum does."

They raced out of the house and
Paul's mother stared after them,
baffled. "I'm glad they're happy. I
don't understand what's going on, but
you're obviously doing well, Sophy."

"I haven't finished yet," Sophy
muttered. She still had one case to
settle. The problem of the pig with
spots.

Maria was still standing in front of the mirror, with her back to the rest of the room. Sophy had a nasty feeling that there was going to be trouble when she turned round.

She went up behind her and spoke quietly in her ear. "I'm sorry, Maria. I don't think the cover-up cream is going to work after all. Not with all those spots. And even if it did –"

"Oh, don't be *silly*, Sophy!" Maria whirled round. There was a look of utter happiness on her face. "Don't you see? This is marvellous!"

"It is?" Sophy blinked.

"Of course it is. I've got chickenpox. I don't have to be a pig at all!"

Maria hugged Sophy, kissed her firmly on both cheeks and danced out of the room, singing at the top of her voice.

"Well!" Paul's mother said. "I hope you've had chickenpox already, Sophy."

"What?" muttered Sophy. She felt stunned. "No, I don't think I have."

"You could be in for a few weeks off school, then." Paul's mother sat down in the big armchair. "Never mind. Sit down and get your breath back."

Sophy sat down, still dazed. Ten minutes before, she had been in deep, deep trouble. Surrounded by people who expected her to solve their problems. And now, magically, all the problems had vanished.

"Chocolate cake?" said Paul's mother. She held out the plate. "Those boys haven't left much, but we might as well finish off what there is."

Mechanically, Sophy took a slice of cake and bit into it. It was moist and sweet, and it tasted deliciously of chocolate.

But she couldn't help noticing that the icing was lumpy.

She put the cake down on the plate and looked at Paul's mother. "My mum's —"

My mum's icing never has lumps. That

was what she meant to say. She was going to offer to copy out Mum's recipe. Just to be helpful.

But at that moment there was a burst of laughter from the football team, in the kitchen. Suddenly Sophy remembered being chased by them. *And* Natalie. *And* Maria. Thirteen people racing after her, because she'd promised to solve their problems. Just to be helpful.

"Yes?" said Paul's mother. "What about your mum?"

Sophy picked up the cake and swallowed it in one gulp. "My mum's expecting me home," she said quickly. "Thanks for the cake. It was lovely. 'Bye."

She leaped out of the room and raced towards the alley, frowning. The poster was still on her front gate.

Suppose hundreds more people had seen it? Suppose there was a long queue outside the door? Suppose –

She couldn't face any more problems. But how could she turn them away without looking ridiculous?

There *had* to be an answer.

By the time she got home she was grinning. She went straight upstairs to find a clean piece of paper. And ten minutes later, there was a new poster on the front gate.

RENT-A-GENIUS
CLOSED
(TO PREVENT THE SPREAD
OF CHICKENPOX)

Tales of Polly and the Hungry Wolf

Catherine Storr

The wolf is no match for clever Polly!

The wolf is up to his old habit of trying to trick Polly so that he can gobble her up. He has thought of several new ways of getting her into his clutches but Polly is too clever to allow herself to be caught by a stupid wolf and she outwits him at every turn!

Also in Young Puffin

The ELM STREET Lot

Philippa Pearce .

"Off to mischief, I suppose?"

Mr Crackenthorpe was a surly old fellow, but he might have been forgiven for his suspicions. For the Elm Street gang were always in on the action, whether they were tracking down a lost hamster, being galley-slaves in a brand-new bathtub, or going on safari across the roof-tops!

READ MORE IN PUFFIN

For children of all ages, Puffin represents quality and variety – the very best in publishing today around the world.

For complete information about books available from Puffin – and Penguin – and how to order them, contact us at the appropriate address below. Please note that for copyright reasons the selection of books varies from country to country.

On the worldwide web: www.puffin.co.uk

In the United Kingdom: Please write to *Dept. EP, Penguin Books Ltd, Bath Road, Harmondsworth, West Drayton, Middlesex UB7 0DA*

In the United States: Please write to *Consumer Sales, Penguin USA, P.O. Box 999, Dept. 17109, Bergenfield, New Jersey 07621-0120*. VISA and MasterCard holders call 1-800-253-6476 to order Penguin titles

In Canada: Please write to *Penguin Books Canada Ltd, 10 Alcorn Avenue, Suite 300, Toronto, Ontario M4V 3B2*

In Australia: Please write to *Penguin Books Australia Ltd, P.O. Box 257, Ringwood, Victoria 3134*

In New Zealand: Please write to *Penguin Books (NZ) Ltd, Private Bag 102902, North Shore Mail Centre, Auckland 10*

In India: Please write to *Penguin Books India Pvt Ltd, 706 Eros Apartments, 56 Nehru Place, New Delhi 110 019*

In the Netherlands: Please write to *Penguin Books Netherlands bv, Postbus 3507, NL-1001 AH Amsterdam*

In Germany: Please write to *Penguin Books Deutschland GmbH, Metzlerstrasse 26, 60594 Frankfurt am Main*

In Spain: Please write to *Penguin Books S. A., Bravo Murillo 19, 1° B, 28015 Madrid*

In Italy: Please write to *Penguin Italia s.r.l., Via Felice Casati 20, I-20124 Milano.*

In France: Please write to *Penguin France S. A., 17 rue Lejeune, F-31000 Toulouse*

In Japan: Please write to *Penguin Books Japan, Ishikiribashi Building, 2-5-4, Suido, Bunkyo-ku, Tokyo 112*

In South Africa: Please write to *Longman Penguin Southern Africa (Pty) Ltd, Private Bag X08, Bertsham 2013*